THE SCIENCE FAIR DISASTER

Written and Illustrated

by

Jan Lister Caldwell

Menagerie Publishing

This is a work of fiction. Unless otherwise indicated, all the names, characters, businesses, places, events and incidents in this book are either the product of the author's imagination or used in a fictitious manner. Any resemblance to actual persons, living or dead, or actual events is purely coincidental.

First Edition 0-9681269-5-2, August 2004, Menagerie Publishing
First published and copyrighted in a collection, Animal Tales, A Collection of Short Stories for Children, by Jan Lister, ISBN 0-9699520-7-4 1996, Menagerie Publishing

ISBN 978-1-7774357-4-5
E-book ISBN 978-1-7774357-5-2

Dedication

When the first edition was published, I was working as an aid and Supply Teacher at St. Stephen Elementary School in my home town. I am keeping that original dedication and adding one, as since that time, I became 'Grandma' to two wonderful granddaughters.

For Keira and Kjersten
I love you to the moon and back!

And
For Judy Q., Lisa M., Patti H.,
& Jeannie L.
You are the best!

Chapter One

Eric Townes was just putting the finishing touches on his display. The sign on the small cage said:

He placed a cardboard maze beside the cage and propped his poster up behind it. It explained what he had learned from his project on how hamsters can learn. His older brother, George, had helped him make the maze from a cardboard box and strips of cardboard, making little trails that led all around inside the box. Some were dead ends. Some led to other trails and eventually ended up where he had put a little hamster treat.

He and his brother had fun putting 'Lightning' at the beginning of the maze and watched him work his way through. The cardboard walls were tall enough that Lightning couldn't climb or even see over them so he had to keep moving until he found his way to the treat.

After a while, he knew his way and didn't take any wrong turns. When he did that several times, Eric and George knew the project was ready for the science fair. Eric was excited and hoped the other kids would vote his project the most interesting display. George won the year he was in grade four and Eric wanted to be able to show off his own big blue ribbon saying 'First Place'.

Grades Three, Four, and Five were all setting up their displays and experiments in the gym for the science fair that afternoon and the competition was really tough. The teachers had made sure they all knew it was important to learn something from working with their projects and to have fun doing them. They kept telling them winning the prize for the most popular display wasn't the most important thing but it was to Eric. He wanted that prize.

For two years he had looked at George's big, blue ribbon. Their mom had put it in a special frame and it hung on the wall next to the stand where their dad's bowling trophies sat. He just had to have that blue ribbon.

Eric placed his reddish brown and white

hamster in the maze for a practice run while some of the other children crowded around to watch.

"Why did you call him 'Lightning'?" asked one of the boys. "Because he is so fast?"

"No," Eric said. "He is pretty fast but see his back?" and he pointed to the zigzag white mark just behind his neck. "It looks like a lightning bolt."

Lightning stopped to stand up and sniff at the crowd. He couldn't see very well with his tiny black beady eyes but he could see well enough to know he wasn't in his own cage and he didn't like that. He went back to sniffing the maze and worked his way to get his treat and hopefully get back to bed in the little box inside his cage. He was sleepy in the daytime and would rather be up and playing in his wheel long after Eric was gone to bed.

While Eric was explaining his experiment to the others, Andy Carter reached in and scooped up the startled hamster.

"Put him back!" Eric snapped.

"I'm not hurting him," protested Andy as he patted Lightning.

"Put him back!" Eric repeated. "Can't you read?" He pointed to his 'Do Not Touch' sign. "You're always doing something you shouldn't!"

"Here's your dumb ol' hamster," Andy grumbled as he dropped him back into the maze.

"You're a trouble-maker," Eric told him angrily. "Why don't you go fix your own dumb project?"

"Maybe I will.   Anyway, it's better than a hamster running around in a box," he said as he left.

"What a mean kid!" Eric groaned and his friends agreed, even though Eric had used his own mean words.

He soon forgot about Andy as he wandered around the gym looking at all the other displays. They were all interesting and some of them were really good.

He knew it would be a hard time for any one to win first prize. He just hoped he would and he figured he might have a good chance, as Lightning was one of only two animal displays and Sam's snake didn't really do anything. It just curled up in the aquarium, ignoring everybody. How could that beat something cute and furry?

Sam did have a big cardboard box beside it, though, and that, Eric had to admit, was very good. It was a little model he had made of the jungle, complete with small tree branches for the jungle trees and green crepe paper cut out and taped on them for the leaves. He even had a little rubber snake hanging in one of the trees to show where his snake would live in the jungle and a poster with pictures of snakes eating rats! The other kids really liked that. Well, most of the boys did, anyway. Some of the girls just said it was gross and moved on to other displays.

Eric noticed everybody, girls and boys, loved Lightning. Maybe he could win after all, he thought. He certainly would beat Sam.

Next, he looked at Mary Thompson's paper mâché solar system model. It was great. She had used a refrigerator carton and cut out the front so you could walk right into it. Inside she painted it black and glued glow in the dark stars and sequins all around the inside and hung the paper mâché planets and moons with strings from the top of the box.

The outside of the box was covered with drawings and pictures she printed off the Internet. They were all of different planets and galaxies. Eric had to admit to himself this was a really fantastic display and by the way the other kids were looking at it and acting, they thought so, too.

It was going to be hard to beat this one but he did have something nobody else had – a very cute little hamster that looked back at everyone that looked at him. Nobody else's displays did that! The more Eric thought about it, the more he was sure that ribbon was going to be his!

He wandered around the other displays. There were two volcano displays. They were basically the same, a big mountain with goo gurgling out of the top. It was fun to watch but he didn't think they were prizewinners.

Tammy Johnson's dad worked at a biological station where they studied fish and other animals from the ocean so she naturally thought of doing something that would show a bit of what her father did. She had pictures of lobsters and different kinds of fish. The main part of her display was a small plastic tank of water that she could pour blue mineral oil into to show how water currents work. After she poured in the blue liquid, which she said was supposed to be for really cold, cold water, she would move the little tank this way and that and show how the cold water moves around and sinks to the bottom of the ocean.

Eric thought it was kind of interesting but he noticed she had to keep dumping out the water and going to get more because it kept mixing too much. He didn't think that worked very well and also thought there was no way she would she get as many votes as he would.

He thought he should get back to his own display and get ready for all the kids from the school to come in, class by class. He hurried by Tony Tubb's hot air balloon display.

Tony had made his hot air balloon from a parachute his dad got at an army surplus store. Though his poster showed pictures of full-size hot air balloons and how they were filled with hot air from gas burners, his had a bunch of helium balloons inside it so it could float just the same. It was floating so well it was trying to go to the ceiling but it was tied down with four small ropes. The action figures inside the basket under the balloon seemed to be looking down at everyone.   All the kids around that table were talking about that being really cool.

Tyler Godsoe's family had an egg farm and he had posters about eggs, what they looked like inside, and photos from his farm right from when the chicks hatched to when they laid the eggs; how his family gathered them, washed them, separated them by size, and then put them in the boxes to send to the stores. He had lots of eggs of all different sizes set up on his table.

The next one was even better, thought Eric. Tamara Spinney was in Grade Five so was allowed to have an electric burner at her table. She had a clear glass pot of water boiling and the steam was turning the turbines of a small steam engine she had put together from a model kit. She had a poster, too, with photos and drawings of the first steam engines and the ones being used today.

Eric had to again admit to himself there were a lot of great experiments and displays. He also had to admit to himself having a very cute little pet might not be enough to win that blue ribbon.

Andy wasn't at his display as he walked quickly by. He did give it a quick glance. *No competition,* he thought. Andy just had a big battery, a light bulb, an on/off switch, and wires to hook them all together. He had it set up for the kids to turn the light on and off so they could see how a flashlight works.

Eric thought it was interesting, though if

anyone had asked him, he would never have said so. Andy even had a small poster to show how electric currents work and how switches turn things on and off, but Eric didn't think the pictures were drawn very well and felt no one would vote for Andy's display.

Eric knew Andy just wasn't liked. He kept to himself a lot, didn't talk to the other kids much, and didn't have any friends it seemed. When Andy first moved here to live with his grandparents, he did talk to the kids, usually about his father working in the Arctic and Antarctica most of the time.

He told lots of stories about his father being a pilot and flying in to rescue people in the deadly cold places of the earth and about how he could race with dog teams and usually won. He told them he had learned to race the dogs, too, and had even worked the controls of his father's plane once but after his mother died, his father wasn't home enough to take care of him and had sent him to live with his grandparents.

Nobody ever believed any of the stories Andy told. They just seemed too fantastic and figured he was just telling lies and bragging and they told him so.

After a while they didn't even believe he had a father because no one ever saw anyone but his grandparents in the six months Andy had lived here. He got teased a lot about being a liar so lately Andy didn't even talk to the kids unless he was telling them to get out of his way.

No, Eric thought, he knew no one liked Andy so he didn't have a chance at that blue ribbon no matter how interesting his display was.

He hurried by the paper towel testing display. It wasn't bad, he thought, but it was more like a commercial on TV. Jimmy had several different brands of paper towels he was getting the kids to test, wetting the towels and then trying to hold apples on them to see if they fell through the wet spot.

The kids thought it was really good when they could get more than one apple on the paper towel and they roared when the apples fell through and rolled all over the floor. Still, Eric didn't think Jimmy was any threat to his winning that ribbon.

Chapter Two

Eric could picture that beautiful ribbon in its own frame right next to his brother's. He just had to have it. It was the most important thing in the world to him. It was all he could think of since his teacher told them they were to make something special for the science fair. Actually, winning that blue ribbon was something he had planned on since George brought home his prize when he was in Grade Four.

When he finally got back to his own display, his mouth dropped open in shock.

"Lightning is gone!!" he squealed. He was in a panic as he dug through the cedar shavings, hoping the hamster was only hiding but he had a sinking feeling he wouldn't find him.

"I bet Andy took him," one of his friends said as he ran over. Some of the others that gathered around him agreed.

Eric's eyes narrowed as he thought about it. "Where is he?" he said angrily.

They looked around and spotted Andy watching Sam McDonald's display, Sam's pet Boa Constrictor. Eric stormed over with three of his friends tagging behind.

He shook his fist in Andy's face. "You took my hamster! Give him back!"

Andy looked surprised. "I haven't got him," said

Andy, sounding a bit angry himself now. He stepped away from the aquarium to face Eric. It was then Eric and his friends saw the snake. It had a large hamster-size lump behind its head!

Eric's eyes bugged out in horror. "Lightning!!" he gasped. He couldn't move. He felt frozen to that spot, staring at the snake and that horrible lump!

"Andy fed Eric's hamster to the snake!" yelled Eric's friends all at the same time.

Everyone crowded around. Someone called out that they ought to go find a teacher. There had been one watching the electric burner but he had to step out a moment and they weren't sure where he went.

"I saw Andy put something in with the snake when Sam was gone," said one of the girls.

Eric exploded. "You did it! You took my hamster! You fed him to the snake! How could you do that?! That is the worst thing you could ever do!!" With that, Eric shoved Andy and nearly pushed him down.

Andy shoved him back. "I didn't do it!!" he shouted.

"Did!" Eric said, poking his finger hard into Andy's shoulder.

"Didn't!" Andy repeated and poked him back.

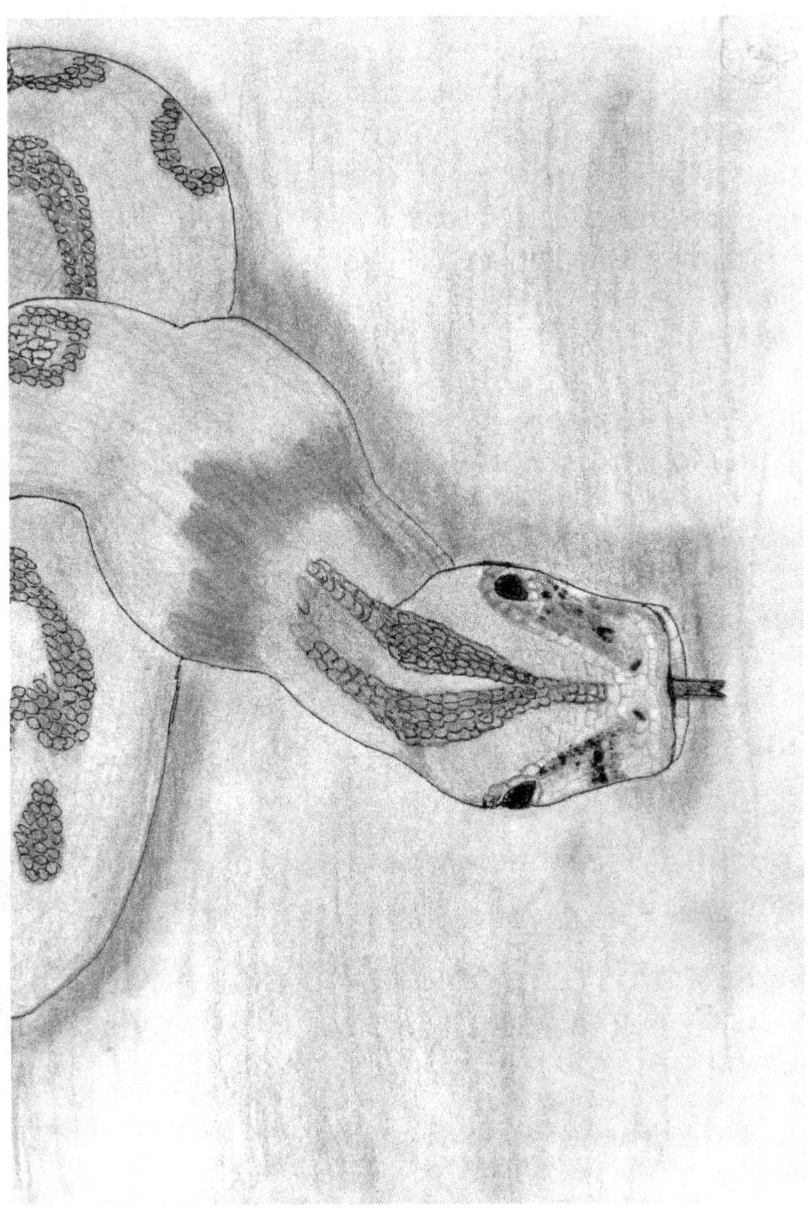

"You guys are going to get into trouble if you fight," one of Eric's friends warned. "Remember what Miss Blake told us when she set up the peace table in our homeroom. If we have trouble, we have to sit down at the peace table and just talk, hands on the table so nobody is hitting or grabbing, and we have to ask questions to see why we're having trouble."

"Stay out of it, Gerry," Eric warned. "We can't talk ourselves out of this trouble. He was seen putting my hamster in with the snake and he can't just say he's sorry for it and no way am I going to say it's okay!"

"Andy says he didn't do it and it was only 'something' that was put in with the snake. Nobody saw the hamster," Gerry reminded him, trying hard to be a peacemaker as Miss Blake had taught them. "Fighting will only make things worse."

"Stay out of it!" Eric warned again and shot him an angry glare.

He poked Andy hard in the shoulder with his finger. Andy winced but tried hard to pretend it didn't hurt and pinched Eric's arm.

By this time the kids were all yelling and some had run out in the hall after a teacher.

The two boys kept shoving and poking. Finally,

Eric's hot temper got the better of him. Shoving just wasn't enough. He grabbed an egg from Tyler Godsoe's table and smashed it hard on the top of Andy's head. The children shrieked. They couldn't believe what was happening!

Andy quickly wiped away the egg that was dripping down into his eyes and snatched up another two. "See how you like it!" he said, smashing them on either side of Eric's face.

Eric fumed silently as the egg ran down his face and under his shirt collar. He looked around until he spotted a large jar of blue mineral oil from Tammy's water current display. He grabbed it and emptied it over Andy's head.

"Yuck!" Andy shivered as the cold slippery goo ran down all over him.

While Eric and his friends stood laughing, Andy snatched the bottle of red water from Steven Jacob's volcano display. "Laugh at this!" he said as he emptied the bottle over Eric's head

By then, the children that went looking for a teacher had found the science teacher getting a drink of water from the cooler in the office. They all rushed back to the gym together.

"I can't leave you people alone for a minute!" he yelled as he ran in. "Look at this mess!!!"

"Andy fed my hamster to Sam's snake!" Eric whined.

Mr. Larkin stopped dead in his tracks in shock at what Eric had said. He stared at the Boa. The lump had slowly made its way toward the middle of the snake.

Chapter Three

"He could still be alive!" someone yelled. "Cut the snake open and save Lightning!"

"NO!!!" Sam threw himself over the top of the aquarium. "Nobody is killing 'Slick'!"

"You've got to save Lightning!" Eric tugged on Mr. Larkin's arm. "You've got to do something!" he pleaded.

"Maybe you could squeeze him out," suggested one of the girls.

"Yeah, like a tube of toothpaste!" added another.

Sam's mouth dropped open. He held onto the tank even more tightly while whining, "NOOOOOOOOOOO!"

Several kids yelled, "Call 911!"

Mr. Larkin didn't know what to do. He could only shake his head in shock and stare at the lump as it slowly worked its way down the snake's long body.

"What is all this noise?!"

The Principal, Mr. Reader, had come running in. Everyone tried to answer at the same time as he hurried over to Mr. Larkin. Just as he got to them, he stepped in some of the egg from the fight and skidded on one foot across the gym floor. He landed upside down across one of the display tables, knocking it over so it pushed Mary Thompson's papier-mâché solar system model crashing into Tamara Spinney's table. Some of the planets flew off their strings and landed on top of the electric burner and caught fire.

Mary and Tamara's ear-piercing screams were drowned out by the fire alarms that started blaring at the first puff of smoke.

Mr. Reader and Mr. Larkin scrambled for the fire extinguishers on the walls outside the gym but they were too late. The sprinklers came on full blast and the children scrambled to get their displays and posters under the tables to save them from the water.

Mr. Reader rushed to the office to turn the sprinklers and alarms off and used the P.A. system to announce everything was all right, but the teachers in the classrooms were already leading the children out of the building. Before they could turn around and go back in, the fire engines had already arrived. Mr. Reader had forgotten to call to let them know the fire was out.

When the teachers saw the engines, they decided to keep going and get all the children away from the school and the trucks.

The firefighters jumped out of the trucks and grabbed their hoses as everyone pointed to the gym. They ran in, carrying their axes and dragging their hoses behind. Instead of a fire, they were surprised to see only a slightly smoky room full of sopping wet children and wet science projects.

Mr. Reader came running in behind them, waving his hands in the air. "I still don't know what is going on here!"

"Where's the fire?" asked the fire chief.

"It's out!" the children shouted as they pointed to the table with the electric burner.

Eric pulled at the Fire Chief's big, black slicker. "Save Lightning!" he begged and pointed to the snake. "Use your axe to cut Slick in half and let my hamster out!"

Sam had never moved since he'd flung himself across the tank. "NOOOOOO!!!" he screamed. "Nobody touches Slick!"

"It's too late anyway," one of the boys pointed out sadly. "The bump is a lot smaller. He's eaten," he sighed.

Eric looked at the snake. Then he looked at Andy. He roared like a wild tiger and ran for him. Mr. Larkin and Mr. Reader both jumped to stop him but as they did, Mr. Larkin slipped on the wet egg-slimed floor and all four of them landed in a heap.

"Murderer!" shouted Eric angrily. "What did Lighting ever do to you?!"

Even as he sat on the floor, Mr. Reader pulled him back as he lunged for Andy again. Andy remained silent.

Several of the children helped Mr. Reader to his feet but Mr. Larkin just waved them away. He sat there, squinting and trying to wipe the slime off of his glasses. One of the firefighters handed him a roll of wet paper towels from the paper towel-testing project beside Eric's table when out onto Mr. Larkin's lap plopped the hamster.

"LIGHTNING!" screamed everyone at once as Eric quickly snatched him up and put him back in his cage.

"My snake didn't eat him," Sam said, sighing, as he unwrapped himself from around the aquarium. "But what did he eat?" he wondered out loud.

"I fed him an egg," Andy said quietly.

"Why didn't you say so?" Mr. Larkin asked, shocked.

"Why bother?" he said, shrugging his shoulders as he looked at his feet. "Nobody ever believes anything I say."

Everyone was quiet. They knew he was right. No matter what Andy said, the other children never believed him anymore, even if it sounded true. They had started believing he lied about everything so they didn't believe anything he said.

After a while, Andy stopped talking to them at all. When that happened, they all thought he was just too different to be a friend. They stopped talking to him, too, and stopped playing with him.

Mr. Reader bent down so their noses were almost touching. "You owe Andy an apology, young man," he told him sternly.

Eric glared at Andy. "Somebody had to let him out of the cage," he said.

"I didn't," Andy told him.

"Did!" Eric stepped toward him.

"Didn't!" As Andy pulled back his arm to punch, the principal grabbed him by the shirt and swung him away from Eric.

"Look!" someone yelled. "The hamster is getting out!" Two of the cage wires were bent just enough for the hamster to flatten and squeeze between them.

"Andy didn't let him out," several children gasped.

Eric caught Lightning as soon as he was out and put him back in the cage. This time he was careful to bend the wires so he couldn't escape again.

He turned to Andy, obviously embarrassed. "I guess I was wrong," he said to his shoes. "I'm sorry."

Mr. Reader put his hand on Eric's shoulder. "Is that any way to say you are sorry? You aren't even looking in his face. Are you really sorry?"

Eric looked up at Mr. Reader and then at Andy. This time he looked right into Andy's eyes and said, "I am sorry. You didn't do it and I didn't believe you. I'm sorry I started a fight." He reached out his hand to Andy.

Andy shrugged. "Yeah, I guess it is okay," and he took Eric's hand to shake on it.

All the children were sorry about accusing Andy of something he hadn't done and they all felt badly that they never thought he could ever tell the truth. They gathered around him, patting him on the back and saying they were sorry, too.

"Well," Mr. Reader said, "We'll have to straighten up the displays and try to fix the ones that were wrecked before we can go on with our science fair. You two boys will have a lot of work ahead of you because you are going to be staying after school to help with the mess you helped make."

Eric and Andy thought that was fair and really wanted to make up for all the trouble. Eric didn't even care about that blue ribbon any more. Knowing Lightning was safe was all that mattered and anyway, he felt too guilty for all the trouble he caused to want anyone to vote for his display.

Eric and Andy looked at each other. Both were soaking wet. Their clothes were stained with colored gunk and their hair was plastered with eggs. They looked around the room. They were surrounded by wet children and firefighters and Mr. Reader and Mr. Larkin were covered with colored egg-slime. They even had eggshells stuck in their hair.

In spite of all the terrible things that had happened, and in spite of all the trouble they were in for fighting and wrecking displays, something good had happened.

Andy didn't feel alone anymore. The other kids were acting like friends again. That is when Andy and Eric started to laugh. They were so glad not to be mad anymore and everyone, including Eric and Andy, looked so ridiculous.

The firefighters broke out laughing next. It was like a flu bug; everyone caught it! All the children started laughing.

Mr. Larkin and Mr. Reader tried their best to look stern but even they had to fight back a snicker or two as they looked at each other.

That was one science fair no one there could ever forget

Note from the Author

When I first wrote this story, I felt something was missing. I have had the honour and privilege of working with wonderful teachers and staff in St. Stephen, New Brunswick, and after spending time with them and the children on a day-to-day basis, I found what I felt was lacking in this story *(first published in a collection of short stories.)* I then turned it into the chapter book you see here.

I want to thank all the teachers I had been working with who had generously given of their time, not only to allow me to read to the children, a great joy for me, but to read and even proofread my stories and give their valuable feedback. It was even read for its reading level and determined it is 'Level L'. I was introduced to the 'Peace Table' at that time, as well. I wish to thank all the schools in my area who have supported my writing.

Look for my science-fiction adventure series, The Bill Little Adventures, available at Amazon and some other online bookstores - in paperback and Kindle.

At the time of this printing, two of the four adventures are available:

Time-Travel Runaway, Book One of the Bill Little Adventures ISBN 9781-7774357-0-7

Only Child, Book Two of the Bill Little Adventures ISBN 978-1-7774357-2-1

www.ingramcontent.com/pod-product-compliance
Lightning Source LLC
Chambersburg PA
CBHW061703050726
47598CB00004B/1645